The Firebird

The Firebird

RETOLD AND ILLUSTRATED BY

MOIRA KEMP

DAVID R. GODINE · Publisher · BOSTON

For Connie

There was once a king who had a beautiful garden planted with many rare and exotic trees. Of them all the rarest was an apple tree which grew in the very middle of the garden. Each morning it was white with blossom, and as the day passed the flowers fell like snow upon the ground. And every day an apple grew and ripened among the leaves, so that by sunset a single golden apple hung on the tree. But it always disappeared during the night, and nobody knew how.

The king was greatly distressed by all this. He sent for his eldest son and said to him,

"Tonight you will keep watch in the garden, and if you catch the thief who steals my golden apples, I will give you half of my kingdom."

When evening came, the eldest prince buckled on his sword, slung his crossbow over his shoulder and went into the garden to keep watch. He sat down under the apple tree and waited. Before long he began to feel sleepy, and soon he stretched out and fell fast asleep. When he awoke in the morning the apple was gone.

The prince went to his father and said,

"I watched all night, but there was no thief. The apple just vanished into thin air."

The king found this difficult to believe, so he sent for his second son. To him too he promised half of his kingdom if he should catch the thief of the golden apples.

As soon as it grew dark, the second prince took his sword and crossbow and went to keep watch. But he was no more successful than his brother. He was soon sound asleep under the tree and when he awoke in the morning the apple was gone.

"Did you see the thief?" his father asked.

"There was no-one," the prince replied. "The apple disappeared all by itself."

Again the king did not find this easy to believe. And when his youngest son asked if he might keep watch, he said,

"But you are so young. How can you hope to succeed where your brothers have failed? But try if you wish. Half of my kingdom will be yours if you catch the thief."

That evening the youngest prince took his sword and crossbow and the skin of a hedgehog and went to keep watch in the garden. He sat under the apple tree with the hedgehog skin across his knees. Whenever he started to fall asleep, the sharp spines pierced his hands and he sprang awake.

Suddenly, at midnight, the whole garden was filled with light as a beautiful bird, with radiant golden plumage and eyes like emeralds perched on the apple tree. The prince took careful aim and, just as the bird was about to take a bite from the golden apple, he let fly an arrow at her shimmering tail. The bird flew away unharmed, but one golden feather, like a flame in the darkness, floated to the ground.

In the morning the prince told the king what had happened and gave him the golden feather. The king was enchanted by it, for its brilliance could fill even the darkest room with a glow of golden light. "You have seen the legendary Firebird," the king said to his youngest son.

The Firebird did not return to the garden and, although the golden apples now hung untouched upon the tree, the king became sick at heart so great was his longing to possess the beautiful creature.

Finally the king called his three sons to him and said,

"My sons, I have grown sad and ill through my longing to see this marvellous bird and to hear her song. To whichever of you brings her back to me alive I will give half my kingdom and he alone will reign after my death."

At once the three princes took leave of their father and rode off in search of the Firebird. When they reached a crossroads they agreed to part company.

"But which road shall each of us take?" asked the eldest brother.

"You choose whichever roads you wish," said the youngest. "And I will take the one that is left."

His brothers agreed to this and each chose a path. Then the second brother said,

"We need a sign in case one of us finds the Firebird. Let us each plant a twig, then if one should take root and grow, it will mean the Firebird has been found."

So the three brothers each planted a twig and rode off in different directions.

The eldest prince rode until he reached the top of a hill. There he dismounted to eat the food he had brought with him. As he was eating, a little vixen crept up to him and said,

"Won't you please give me something to eat? I am so very hungry."

But the prince fired an arrow at her from his crossbow and she disappeared.

The second prince rode until he came to the edge of a wide plain where he stopped to eat. Here a little vixen crept up to him and asked for something to eat. But he too sent an arrow flying after the vixen and she vanished.

The youngest prince rode until he came to a river. He was tired and hungry, so he tethered his horse to a tree and sat down by the river to eat. As he ate he saw a little vixen creep closer and closer to him.

"Won't you please give me something to eat?" the vixen said. "I am so very hungry."

The prince said, "There is plenty here for both of us." And he divided his food equally and gave one half of it to the vixen. When she had eaten her fill, she said,

"You have shared your meal with me and in return I shall help you. If you follow me and do everything I say, the Firebird will be yours."

Immediately the vixen set off ahead of the prince, running like the wind through forests and meadows, brushing aside trees and rocks with great sweeps of her flame-coloured tail, bridging rivers and clearing a path over mountains and through valleys. The prince galloped behind her until at last he saw a castle of copper glinting in the distance.

"The Firebird is in this castle," said the vixen. "You must enter at noon when the guards are asleep. Make your way to a hall where you will find the Firebird asleep on her perch. There will be two cages hanging on the wall, one of gold and one of wood. Be sure to put her in the wooden cage. If you don't you will regret it."

The prince stole into the castle past the sleeping guards and found everything just as the vixen had described. The Firebird did not even open her eyes when he lifted her off her perch and put her into the wooden cage. But then he caught sight of the golden cage and thought,

"This wooden cage is not worthy of such a beautiful bird." So he took the Firebird out of the wooden cage and put her into the golden one.

Suddenly the Firebird awoke and let out such a piercing cry that she woke the guards who rushed into the hall, seized the prince and dragged him before the King of the Copper Castle.

"How dare you sneak into my castle and try to steal my Firebird," the King said angrily.

"I am not a thief, your Majesty," replied the prince. "Please hear my story before you judge me. In my father's garden there grows an apple tree that bears one golden apple each day. Every night your Firebird would come and steal the apple. One night I took a golden feather from her tail. And when my father saw it he grew sick with longing to see the Firebird herself. Now I fear that only the sight of her will restore him to health."

"If you had asked me, I would have given you the bird most willingly," the King replied. "But now you may have her only if you succeed in bringing me the Horse with the Golden Mane."

The prince returned sadly to the vixen and told her what had taken place.

"You see what happens when you do not do as I tell you," the vixen said. "But do not despair. I shall help you to find the Horse with the Gold Mane."

Once again she ran ahead of the prince, clearing a path with her bushy tail. And the prince galloped behind until at last they came in sight of a castle of silver.

"In this castle you will find the Horse with the Golden Mane," said the vixen. "Enter the castle at noon when the guards are asleep and go straight to the stables. You will find the Horse with the Golden Mane. Hanging on the wall will be two bridles, one of gold and one of leather. You must be sure to take the plain leather one. You will be sorry if you do not."

The prince crept into the castle and found everything just as the vixen had told. The Horse with the Golden Mane was eating live coals from a silver trough. The prince slipped the leather bridle over the horse's head, and was just about to lead him away when he saw the golden bridle and thought,

"Only a golden bridle is worthy of such a beautiful horse." And he replaced the plain leather bridle with the one of gold.

As soon as the Horse with the Golden Mane sensed the gold bridle about his head, he began to neigh and stamp his hooves and made such a noise that he woke the guards who rushed in, seized the prince and dragged him before the King of the Silver Castle.

"How dare you sneak into my castle and try to steal my Horse with the Golden Mane," the King said angrily.

"Please hear my story, your Majesty," the prince pleaded, "before you judge whether or not I am a thief."

And the prince told the King how he feared that his father would die if he did not return home with the Firebird, which he could only do if he took the Horse with the Golden Mane to the King of the Copper Castle.

"I would have given you my horse if you had asked for him openly," said the King. "But now I will only part with him if you bring me the Princess with the Golden Hair."

The prince returned sadly to the vixen and told her what had happened.

"I do not know why I should help you when you pay no attention to what I say," the vixen said. "However, I will help you once more and take you to the Princess with the Golden Hair."

Again the vixen ran in front of the prince, clearing a path for him with great sweeps of her tail. At last they came to the sea at the very edge of the world. There a castle of gold stood glittering in the sunlight.

"In this castle lives the Queen of the Sea with her three daughters,"

said the vixen. "The youngest daughter is the Princess with the Golden Hair. Go to the Queen and ask for her daughter's hand in marriage. When she asks you to choose from among the three princesses, be sure to choose the girl who is wearing the plainest dress."

So the prince went to the Queen of the Sea and asked if he might marry the Princess with the Golden Hair. The Queen led him into a room where her three lovely daughters sat spinning. But it was impossible to tell them apart for they were identical in every respect, and each girl's hair was hidden by a veil. Only their clothes were different.

They were all dressed in white, but the gown and veil of one were woven with golden thread, and in her hand she held a golden distaff. Another wore a gown and veil embroidered with silver thread and she held a silver distaff. The third princess wore a plain white gown and her distaff was made of wood.

"Now you must choose," said the Queen. The prince did not hesitate and he pointed to the princess dressed in plain white.

"You have chosen well," said the Queen. "But tomorrow you must choose again." The Queen suspected that someone had helped him.

That night the prince could not sleep. He did not know how he was to make the right choice next day. As the sun began to rise, he got up and went to walk in the garden. Suddenly a girl dressed all in white stood before him.

"If you want to recognise me today," she said, "look for the little fly that will be buzzing round my head." Then she disappeared.

Later that morning the Queen took the prince to her three daughters. This time they all wore identical dresses and each girl's hair was hidden by a veil.

"Now you must decide which of my daughters is the girl you chose yesterday," the Queen said.

It was impossible to tell them apart, and the prince looked in despair from one to the other. He had nearly given up hope when a little fly came buzzing into the room and flew around one of the princesses.

"This is the one I choose," said the prince decisively.

The Queen was furious. She was now quite certain that someone was helping the prince.

"You have chosen correctly," she said. "But I do not think you will find your next task so easy." Then she gave the prince a small golden sieve and said,

"In the garden is a lake. You must empty it with this sieve before sunset. If you fail in this task, you will lose not only my daughter but your life as well."

The prince took the sieve and went to the edge of the lake. When he tried to fill the sieve, all the water ran out through the holes. It was an impossible task. So he sat down by the lake and wondered what to do next. Suddenly the girl appeared and her hair, as golden as the sun, hung loose about her shoulders.

"Why are you so sad?" she asked.

"Your mother has set me an impossible task," replied the prince. "So now I will never win your hand."

"Let me help you," said the princess. And she took the sieve and threw it into the middle of the lake. The water began to boil and foam until a thick mist engulfed the whole garden.

Almost at once they heard the sound of hooves, and from the mist came the little vixen leading the prince's horse.

The prince lifted the princess onto his horse, climbed up behind her and they rode off as fast as they could. This time the vixen followed behind, breaking down bridges and tearing up trees and rocks with great sweeps of her bushy tail. As she raced over mountains and through valleys, she destroyed the path she had made, and put back everything as it had been before.

Soon they were in sight of the silver castle. But the prince was sad for he loved the beautiful princess and did not want to exchange her for the Horse with the Golden Mane.

"Do not worry," said the vixen. "I have helped you before and I will not fail you now." And she took a tremendous leap into the air, turned a somersault and transformed herself into a girl who looked exactly like the Princess with the Golden Hair.

"Leave the princess here," said the vixen, "and take me to the castle in her place."

The King of the Silver Castle was delighted with the princess and gave the prince the Horse with the Golden Mane in exchange.

At once the prince returned to where the real princess waited, and they rode away as fast as they could.

Meanwhile the king ordered a great feast to celebrate his marriage to the Princess with the Golden Hair. The king proposed a toast to his new bride. "To the loveliest girl in the world."

Suddenly one of the courtiers leaped to his feet and said, "Lovely she may be, but she has the eyes of a fox!"

Everyone turned to look at the princess. She was no longer there. A vixen sat in her place beside the king. Before anyone could move, the vixen leaped over the table and out through the open window. As she ran she destroyed the path she made so that the king's guards could find no trace of the way she had gone.

When she caught up with the prince and princess they were already within sight of the copper castle. But the prince looked sad for he did not want to part with the Horse with the Golden Mane.

"Leave everything to me," said the vixen, and she took a tremendous leap into the air, turned a somersault and transformed herself into a horse with a golden mane.

"Now take me to the copper castle," she said.

The King of the Copper Castle was delighted with the horse, and in exchange he gave the prince the Firebird in her golden cage.

At once the prince returned to the princess and the real Horse with the Golden Mane, and they rode off together as fast as they could.

The king was very proud of his new horse, so he invited his courtiers to come and see him.

"He is a very fine horse indeed," said one of the courtiers. "But it seems to me he has the tail of a fox."

All eyes turned towards the Horse with the Golden Mane. But he was no longer there. Instead they saw a vixen leap through the open stable door and run like the wind. The guards tried to follow her, but she destroyed the path as before.

When the vixen caught up with the prince and princess they were resting by the banks of the river where she had first met the prince.

"It is time for us to say farewell," the vixen said. "You have the Firebird and no longer need my help. Go home and live in peace and happiness with your princess. But do not linger on the way, or you will regret it." With that she disappeared among the trees.

The prince went on his way. Beside him on the Horse with the Golden Mane was the Princess with the Golden Hair. And he carried the Firebird in her golden cage. He thought himself the happiest of men.

When he came to the crossroads where he had parted company with his brothers, he found that the twig he had planted had taken root and had grown into a fine tree. His brothers' twigs had withered and died.

The prince and princess were tired after their long journey, so he tied both horses to the tree and hung the cage from one of its branches. Then he and the princess lay down and were soon fast asleep.

While they were sleeping, the young prince's brothers arrived at the crossroads. When they saw that their brother had found not only the Firebird, but a beautiful princess and a magnificent horse as well, their hearts were filled with hatred and envy.

"If our brother returns home with the Firebird," they whispered, "he will be given half of our father's kingdom, and one day he will succeed our father to the throne. But if we were to kill him here, one of us could take the Princess with the Golden Hair, and the other the Horse with the Golden Mane. We could both give the Firebird to our father and share the kingdom between us."

With this they killed their young brother as he lay sleeping, and they threatened to kill the princess too if she ever dared to tell anyone what they had done.

When they returned home, the princess was given fine clothes and jewels to wear, and she was shown to the best room in the palace where ladies waited to attend to her every need. But she hung her head and wept and spoke no word.

The Horse with the Golden Mane was led to a marble stable. But he too hung his head and would not eat.

Then the brothers gave their father the Firebird, but she gave him no pleasure. The radiance of her beautiful golden feathers was dimmed and she hid her head beneath her wing and refused to sing. And when the king could obtain no news of his youngest son he grew sadder and sadder until at last he took to his bed and lay there pale and motionless.

The prince's body lay under the tree for many days. Then one day the little vixen happened to pass by and discovered him. She gently nuzzled his face, but even she could not bring him back to life. Suddenly she saw a raven with two of her young flying above the body. She hid behind a bush and as soon as one of the young ravens flew down to feed on the body, she leaped out and caught the bird in her sharp claws. The mother raven flew down onto a branch of the tree and cried,

"Kraaar, kraaar! Please do not harm my child. He has done nothing to you, and if you let him go I will help you."

"Then listen, mother raven," said the vixen, "I will free your child if you fly to the ends of the earth and bring me back some of the water of life and the water of death."

For three days and three nights the vixen waited. On the fourth day the raven returned carrying two bottles, one containing the water of life and the other the water of death.

The vixen took the bottles. Then she tore the young raven in two and sprinkled his body with the water of death. Immediately the young raven's body grew together. Then she sprinkled it with the water of life, and he flapped his wings and flew back to his mother. At once she sprinkled the water of death on the young prince, and his body grew together without a scar. Then she sprinkled him with the water of life, and he jumped to his feet and cried, "What a long time I have been asleep!"

"Yes and but for me," said the vixen, "you might have slept forever. Because you ignored my advice, your brothers killed and robbed you while you lay sleeping under this tree. But I can no longer help you. You will have to win back your treasures alone." Before they parted company, she gave him an old tunic to wear instead of his blood-stained rags.

The prince continued his journey home. When he arrived at his father's castle and asked for work no one recognized him dressed in a poor man's clothes, and he was given a job as a stable-boy.

One day he overheard two of the grooms talking about the beautiful horse with a golden mane which was wasting away because he refused to eat.

"Give him some pea-straw," said the prince. "I'm sure he will eat that."

The boys burst out laughing. "Not even our cart-horses would eat such rubbish," they said.

But the prince fetched a bundle of pea-straw and put it into the horse's marble trough. Then he stroked his lovely mane and whispered, "Why are you so sad? Your master has returned." The horse recognized the prince's voice at once, neighed with joy and began to eat the straw.

Everyone in the palace began talking about the stable-boy who had cured the Horse with the Golden Mane. Soon the news reached the king himself and he sent for the boy.

"Perhaps you could help the Firebird too," he said.

"She is so sad that she will not sing or even eat. If she dies, I will die too."

"Give me some barley-husks, your Majesty," said the boy, "and she will sing for you with all her heart."

The servants laughed as they went to fetch the barley. "Not even our geese would eat that sort of thing," they said.

But the prince held the barley out to the bird and whispered, "Why are you so sad? Your prince has returned." The Firebird recognized his voice and began to eat. At once life flowed back into her golden feathers, and her brilliant plumage shone with a new radiance. Her green eyes glinted as she spread her tail like a golden fan and opened her beak to pour forth the most glorious song, such a song as had never before been heard in all that land. And as she sang the king felt his strength returning and for the first time in many days he got up from his bed.

"Perhaps you could help the golden-haired maiden too," he said. "She will not speak and she never stops weeping."

"If I could see her, your Majesty," said the prince, "I think I could make her happy again."

So the king took the prince to the room where the Princess with the
Golden Hair sat crying. The prince sat down beside her, took her hands
tenderly in his and said softly, ''Why are you so sad, my beloved? Can't
you see that your prince has returned?''

At once she recognized him and threw her arms about his neck. The
king was amazed to see the princess kissing a stable-boy.

Then the prince turned to him and said, "Father, don't you recognize
me? I am your youngest son." The king was overjoyed to find his son
alive and well and he took him in his arms and wept. Then the prince told

him all that had happened since he had left the castle, and the princess told how his brothers had killed him and had threatened to kill her too if she betrayed them.

The king was so angry to hear of his sons' treachery that he ordered them to be executed. But to his youngest son he gave half of his kingdom.

So the prince married the Princess with the Golden Hair. And when the old king died they ruled wisely and happily together for many years.

First U.S. edition published in 1984 by
David R. Godine, Publisher, Inc.
306 Dartmouth Street, Boston, Massachusetts 02116

First published in 1983 by Hamish Hamilton Children's Books, London

Library of Congress Cataloging in Publication Data
Kemp, Moira
The firebird
Adaptation of: Zhar-ptitsa.
Summary: A king who desires the beautiful Firebird
send his three sons to find and bring her to him.
[1. Folklore – Soviet Union] I. Zhar-ptitsa.
II. Title.
PZ8.1.K355Fi   1984   398.2′454′0947   83-11570
ISBN 0-87923-486-5

Calligraphy by Richard Lipton

First edition printed in Italy by
Arnoldo Mondadori Editore, Verona